MW00913131

Pet Riddles with Franny and Frank

written by
Lisa Eisenberg

illustrated by
Scott Scheidly

HARCOURT BRACE & COMPANY

Orlando Atlanta Austin Boston San Francisco Chicago Dallas New York
Toronto London

My dog ran away!
Did you put up a sign?
Why? My dog can't read!

Where does a dog always have to be quiet?

In a no-barking zone!

What's the first thing my hamster puts in his food?
What?

His front teeth!

Do your fish need new water?
No. They haven't finished their old water yet!

What kind of fish are in the sky?

Starfish!

Carrots are good for your eyes.
How do you know?

Did you ever see a rabbit
with glasses on?

I'm getting some birdseed.
Why? You don't have a bird.

I know, but I want to grow one.

What food does your cat like the best?
Mice Crispies!

My cat ate some yarn.
How is she?
Fine. But she just had mittens!

Oops! I think I just stepped on my cat's foot.
What did she say?

Me-OW
Me-OW!

What did the cat say to the mouse?
"It's nice gnawing you!"